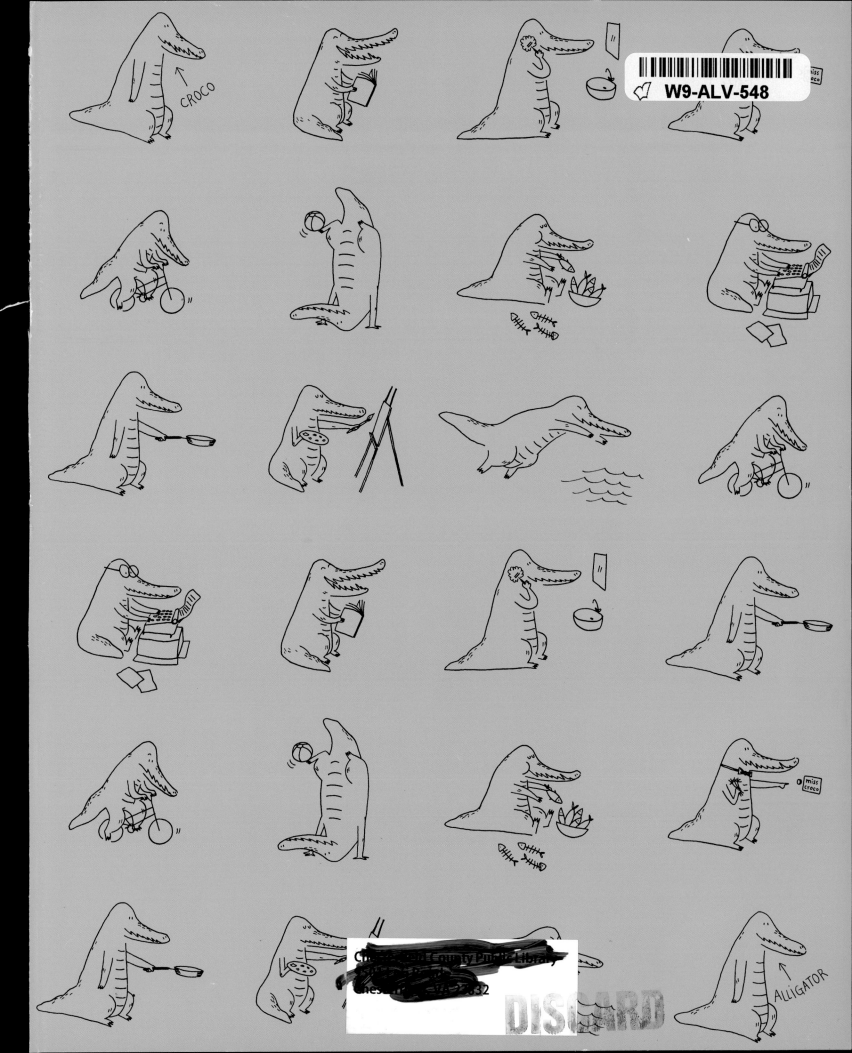

To my mates at the studio

ATHENEUM BOOKS FOR YOUNG READERS

An imprint of Simon & Schuster Children's Publishing Division

1230 Avenue of the Americas, New York, New York 10020

Copyright © 2013 by Éditions Les Fourmis Rouges

English language translation copyright © 2015 by Hannele & Associates

First published in France as *Pedro Crocodile et George Alligator.*

Text and images by Delphine Perret

Hand-lettering of English translations by Emma Ledbetter, in the style of Delphine Perret

All rights reserved, including the right of reproduction in whole or in part in any form.

ATHENEUM BOOKS FOR YOUNG READERS is a registered trademark of Simon & Schuster, Inc.

Atheneum logo is a trademark of Simon & Schuster, Inc.

For information about special discounts for bulk purchases, please contact Simon & Schuster

Special Sales at 1–866–506–1949 or business@simonandschuster.com.

The Simon & Schuster Speakers Bureau can bring authors to your live event. For more information

or to book an event, contact the Simon & Schuster Speakers Bureau at 1–866–248–3049 or

visit our website at www.simonspeakers.com.

Book design by Debra Sfetsios–Conover

The text for this book is set in Soup Bone.

The illustrations for this book are rendered in black felt–tip pen and colored ink.

Manufactured in China

0315 SCP

First US Edition 2015

10 9 8 7 6 5 4 3 2 1

Library of Congress Cataloging–in–Publication Data

Perret, Delphine, author, illustrator.

[Pedro Crocodile et George Alligator]

Pedro and George / words and pictures by Delphine Perret. — First US edition.

pages cm

Originally published in France by Éditions Les Fourmis Rouges in 2013 under title: Pedro Crocodile et

George Alligator.

Summary: "Pedro and George are fed up with the children of the world getting them confused. Pedro

is a crocodile, and George is an alligator. There's a difference, you know. This determined pair

decides to go on a mission to prove who's who, once and for all"—Provided by publisher.

ISBN 978–1–4814–2925–2 (hardcover)

ISBN 978–1–4814–2926–9 (eBook)

[1. Crocodiles—Fiction. 2. Alligators—Fiction. 3. Cousins—Fiction. 4. Humorous stories.] I. Title.

PZ7.P4328Pe 2015

[E]—dc23   2014020003

Pedro
and
George

words and pictures by Delphine Perret

A
atheneum
Atheneum Books for Young Readers
New York   London   Toronto   Sydney   New Delhi

One day, while he was picking his teeth with a fish bone,
Pedro Crocodile heard a knock on his door. It was his
cousin George, the alligator, and he didn't look pleased.

"Fish bone?" Pedro asked politely.

"Listen, Cousin, I'm fed up with everyone calling me a
crocodile. I am an alligator!"

Pedro suggested a little mud bath, and George, who'd had a
long journey with a lot of mosquitoes, agreed.

"You know, it's not my fault if people think you're a crocodile like me," said Pedro.

"Oh, no?"

"No! It's the children on the other end of the world. They confuse us!"

"The world has another end? With children on it?" George was astonished.

"Yes, children who will say all kinds of foolish things!"

George hadn't come across many children in his life.

"Hmm," he said pensively.

"Hmm," Pedro repeated thoughtfully. Then, like a detective, he declared, "I propose we investigate."

"Okeydokey," said George, who was thinking of something else entirely.

So Pedro packed two sandwiches, a comb, and a toothbrush and then slammed the door.

(The comb was of no use, of course. It was only for show.)

On their way, they asked themselves many questions.

"Can children be eaten?"

"Yes, they're a little sweet, but you can eat them."

"And if we did eat them?"

"Well, that would teach them a lesson!"

Pedro wrote it down in his notebook.

"Eat-ing child-ren."

They walked for a long time.

When they arrived in a city at the other end of the world, Pedro Crocodile cleared his throat and said, "Good morning, sir. Would you be kind enough to tell me where we can find children, please?"

"At this hour, you will certainly find some at school."

"Thank you, sir."

"You really know how to talk," George Alligator noted.

At school, in Mrs. Muiche's class, it was time for dictation.

"Miss! Miss!"

"Silence, Josephine, concentrate!"

"But, miss, there is a crocodile biting my foot!"

"My goodness, you'll never stop inventing stories. . . . Let's resume dictation. 'In the cool morning, comma . . .'"

"But, miss! It's true, look at my shoe."

"Ooooohmygoodnessitisnotpossibleitisnot truewhatisthis!"

"Is 'ooooohmygoodnessitisnotpossibleitis nottruewhatisthis!' one word, miss?" asked Claude, who wanted to have a good grade in dictation for once.

While Mrs. Muiche was shouting, Josephine got the one who was biting her foot in a judo hold. (It was George Alligator, who was the first to try and taste a child.)
Pif paf bam!

Pedro Crocodile hid behind the cupboard.

He was finding Josephine a tough nut to crack. He didn't know it, but she had a yellow-orangey belt in judo!

"Good heavens, well done, Josephine!"

THE DOG

Mrs. Muiche had given up shrieking like a car alarm. She squinted her eyes, pursed her lips, and took a breath. "Look, children . . . a croc-o-dile!"

A little voice came from the back of the classroom, near the radiator.

"Oh no, not at all, it is an alligator! The crocodile is the one hiding behind the cupboard."

Theodore crossed the room with the big book of natural science that Granny Zette had given him for his birthday.

Mrs. Muiche said nothing, for once.

He continued in a shrill voice, "Yes, because a crocodile can be recognized by his fourth lower tooth, which sticks out when his mouth is closed."

Pedro Crocodile tried to stand up tall to show the class.

George Alligator tried nothing.

The whole class found the presentation on crocodiles and alligators fascinating and thought that it would be really great if school was like this every day. Even Audrey, the most nearsighted of the class, who didn't see anything but two giant green beans.

Pedro Crocodile displayed his webbed feet, the lumps on his back, and his nostrils, which closed automatically.

The children also admired George Alligator's black eye. They took him to the nurse, where he received a pretty bandage.

Josephine apologized.

At school, the teachers organized Crocodile and Alligator Week. They had several wonderful days full of green crepe paper.

But soon it was time for Pedro and George to return home. They both had a lot to do: sorting toothpicks, shaking out the living room rug, repainting the bathrooms, and visiting old Aunt Juju.

The school gave them two beautiful scooters for their journey back.

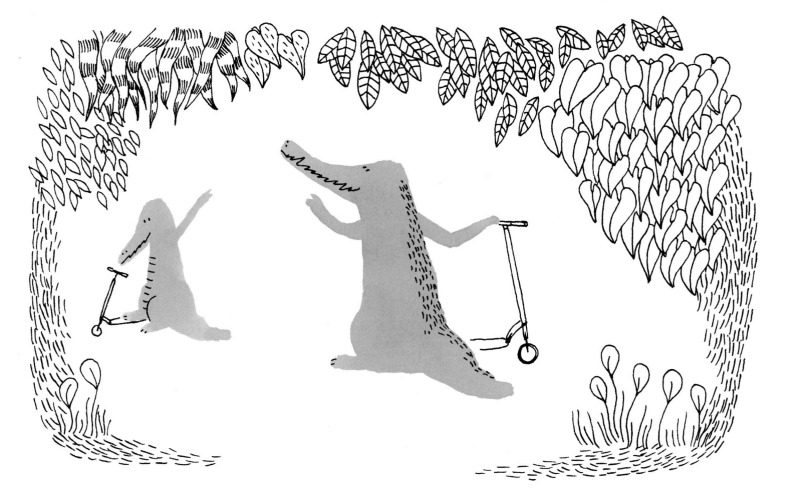

They had a safe trip (despite a gnat that landed in George's eye).

Pedro Crocodile was very happy to be home.
He had a little mud bath. And in the evening, he went to
sleep thinking about the very square teeth of human beings.

A few days later, he received a lovely letter covered in hearts:

Dear Pedro and dear George,

Thank you for coming to school, it was super. I hope you are doing well. Mom bought me new boots (because George chewed up my left shoe). Now I have the most beautiful boots in all the second grade, and even Betty is jealous! And finally, thanks to you, everybody knows the difference between a crocodile and an iguana.

Big kisses,
Josephine

PS I wrote the same exact letter to George a week ago, but he didn't answer. Maybe I have the wrong address?

Tip is not included

Oy! thought Pedro. *I have a feeling I won't have peace for long.*

And who knocked on the door just at that moment? His cousin George.

He didn't look pleased.

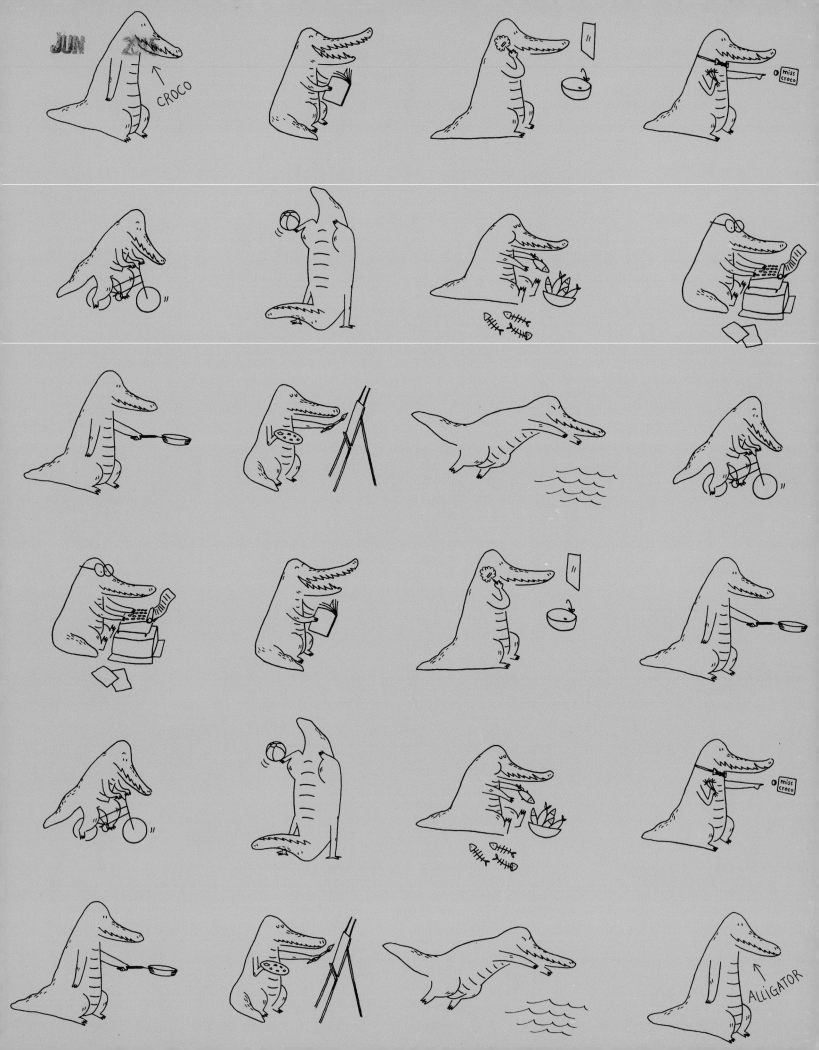